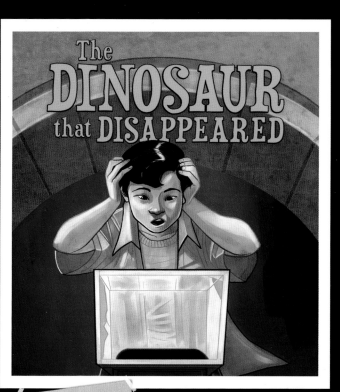

The DINOSAUR that DISAPPEARED

by
Steve Brezenoff

illustrated by
Marcos Calo

f Samantha Archer,

Field Trip Mysteries are published by Stone Arch Books
A Capstone Imprint
1710 Roe Crest Drive
North Mankato, Minnesota 55603
www.capstonepub.com

Library of Congress Cataloging-in-Publication Data
Brezenoff, Steven.
   The dinosaur that disappeared / by Steve Brezenoff ;
illustrated by Marcos Calo.
   p. cm. -- (Field trip mysteries)
   ISBN 978-1-4342-5980-6 (library binding)
   ISBN 978-1-4342-6213-4 (pbk.)
1. School field trips--Juvenile fiction. 2. Natural history museums--Juvenile fiction. 3. Dinosaurs--Juvenile fiction. 4. Chickens--Juvenile fiction. 5. Theft--Juvenile fiction. [1. Mystery and detective stories. 2. School field trips--Fiction. 3. Natural history museums--Fiction. 4. Museums--Fiction. 5. Dinosaurs--Fiction. 6. Chickens--Fiction. 7. Theft--Fiction.] I. Calo, Marcos, ill. II. Title. III. Series: Brezenoff, Steven. Field trip mysteries.
                                                    2012049376

   PZ7.B7576Din 2013
   813.6--dc23

Graphic Designer: Kristi Carlson

Summary: James "Gum" Shoo and his friends are on a trip to the River City Natural History Museum, where they find that a small dinosaur model and some chickens have gone missing.

Printed in China.
032013   007228RRDF13

TABLE OF CONTENTS

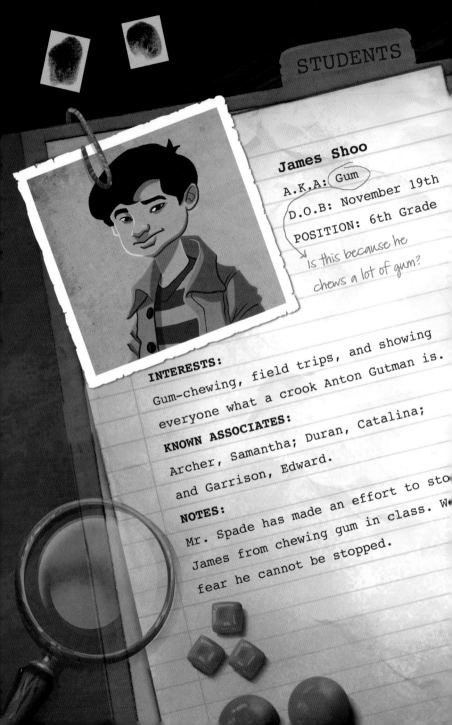

James Shoo

A.K.A: (Gum)

D.O.B: November 19th

POSITION: 6th Grade

Is this because he chews a lot of gum?

INTERESTS:

Gum-chewing, field trips, and showing everyone what a crook Anton Gutman is.

KNOWN ASSOCIATES:

Archer, Samantha; Duran, Catalina; and Garrison, Edward.

NOTES:

Mr. Spade has made an effort to sto James from chewing gum in class. We fear he cannot be stopped.

CHAPTER ONE

THE BUMPY ROAD

I'm James Shoo, but everyone calls me Gum. One Friday morning, my friends Cat, Edward, Sam, and I sat on the school bus, heading toward yet another field trip.

This time, we were off to the River City Natural History Museum in downtown River City.

Egg — that's what we call Edward — loved to take photos. The roads downtown, though, were too bumpy to shoot. "I can't even steady my camera enough to take a picture out the window," he complained.

At a red light, Anton Gutman strolled down the aisle. He should have been in his seat, but he's a rule-breaker.

"Trying to take a photo of that billboard?" he asked smugly.

The four of us looked out Egg's window. High on the nearest building was a big sign with a person's sleeping face lying on a pillow. In big, blue letters, the sign read "Gutman Pillows — for the Best Night's Sleep."

"Yup," Anton said. He grinned like a wolf. "That's my mom's new business. The Gutmans keep getting more famous."

"Wow," said Cat. "Are the pillows really comfy?" Cat's the only one of the four of us who's ever nice to Anton. I suppose that's because she's such a nice person in general.

"Of course they are," Anton snapped. "Do you think my mom's sign would lie?"

Cat smiled and shook her head.

* * *

The River City Natural History Museum looks like a castle made of brown stones. It has giant windows and two huge towers.

We'd all been there lots of times. River City kids visit the museum on field trips almost every year. When I was a little kid, the dinosaurs were cool. But now? It's boring.

"Wow," said a kid behind me as we got off the bus. "What an amazing building!" I was surprised that the building was new to someone.

"It sure is," said another voice. "I can hardly believe it."

Who were these kids? I turned around to see, and there was Cat standing with two sixth graders I didn't recognize.

"Hi, Cat," I said.

"Oh, hello, Gum," she said. "These guys are new."

Cat waved toward a boy with a big, flat bag hanging from his shoulders. "This is Jace," she said. "And this is Harriet." She pointed at a girl in a blue jacket.

"Hi," said Jace. "I can't wait to get inside and sketch some of those dinosaurs."

"Jace is an artist," said Cat, smiling. "And Harriet is going to start an animal rights group at school! I can't wait to join."

Harriet yawned. "Yeah," she said. "The club at my old school held protests. We even marched on the state capital."

"Wow," I said. "You must be pretty committed."

"Obviously," Harriet said. She said good-bye to Cat and followed the rest of the class inside.

"Nice girl," I said to Cat, rolling my eyes. We caught up with the others and went inside.

We followed Mr. Spade and our museum guide, Dr. Flickenflak.

"I know you're all excited to see the dinosaurs," said Dr. Flickenflak.

"Who does she think she's talking to?" I said under my breath to Egg. "Five-year-olds?"

Egg shrugged. "I like dinosaurs," he said.

"Me too," said Cat.

Sam rolled her eyes. "I'm with you, Gum," she said. "Let's hope this field trip gets more interesting soon, if you know what I mean."

I knew what she meant: hopefully there would be a mystery for us to solve.

"Before we get to the dinosaur fossils and models," Dr. Flickenflak went on, "I'd like to show you our newest dinosaur exhibit."

We followed her and Mr. Spade down a new glass hallway at the back of the building. At the other end, there was a set of swinging doors. Colorful decals decorated the hallway. There were parrots and eagles and birds I didn't even recognize, some with long tail feathers, some with great yellow claws, and some with teeth!

"Okay, children," Dr. Flickenflak said when she reached the doors. "Welcome to the new River City Aviary!"

"What's an aviary?" I whispered to Sam. She shrugged.

"An aviary?" said Harriet. "At a natural history museum?"

Cat leaned over and explained, "An aviary is a big place to keep birds in captivity."

"Live birds?" Sam said. "That is weird."

Dr. Flickenflak stood in front of the doors to the aviary. "Such curious children," she said. "Birds are especially interesting to paleontologists because —"

Suddenly, a man in a gleaming, white jumpsuit slammed out of the aviary doors. "Dr. Flickenflak!" he shouted.

"Bernie!" the doctor said. "What is going on?"

"It's terrible!" said Bernie. He pulled out a set of keys and locked the aviary doors.

"What's terrible?" asked Dr. Flickenflak.

"The chickens are gone," said Bernie.

FOWL PLAY

"The chickens are gone?" Cat repeated.

"They probably flew away," I said.

"Flew away?" said Anton. He crossed his arms and sneered at me. "Boy, you sure are dumb."

"Shush, Anton," Egg said. Then he said very quietly, so only I would hear, "Chickens can hardly fly, Gum."

"Really?" I asked, probably a little too loud, because Anton laughed.

"Really," said Dr. Flickenflak. "In fact, many birds, like ostriches, don't fly at all. Some birds, though they cannot fly, are excellent swimmers."

"So," I said, "the chickens swam away?"

My friends groaned at my joke as we walked away from the aviary.

"I still don't get why there's an aviary in the dinosaur exhibit," Harriet said sharply.

"I'm sure the birds are treated well," Cat said.

"Treated well?" Harriet snapped. "How can they be happy? They're cooped up inside this stuffy, old building, instead of flying freely!" She stomped off to the front of the group.

"Or swimming in the sea," I pointed out. "Or walking around."

In the fossil and model rooms, the ceilings were very high — to fit the big dinosaurs inside, I guess. I could hear the class's echoing voices, but I couldn't make out any words. It was just a big mess of shouting and talking.

Only one person was very quiet: Sam.

"Something on your mind?" I asked. "It's about the chickens, isn't it?"

Sam nodded.
"I suspect foul play,"
she said.

I laughed. "Foul play?" I said. "Or *fowl* play?" I laughed some more, but no one else did.

"Ugh," I said. "Jokes are never funny if you have to explain them!" I stomped off toward the room with the really big dinosaurs. My friends followed.

Sam said, "Then don't tell jokes you have to explain." She smiled and patted my back. "Back to the case," she said. "Who would want some chickens?"

"Chuck's Cluck Cluck," Egg said. "Seems like the obvious place."

"Never heard of it," Cat said. "What is it?"

"It's a fried chicken restaurant," I explained. "It's right next door."

Sam tapped her chin. "Interesting idea," she said. "Free chickens to cook and serve."

Cat shuddered. "Oh, gross," she said. "Who would steal chickens from a museum just to cook them? How terrible."

"It is pretty sick," I agreed. "But I don't think it was Chuck's Cluck Cluck. I think it was Anton Gutman."

Sam groaned. "Gum," she said, "why would Anton steal chickens?"

"To be a pain," Egg said.

"There's that," I said. Then I added quietly, "But there's also feathers."

"Feathers," Sam whispered. She snapped and said it again: "Feathers!"

I smiled.

"What am I missing?" Cat said. "What do feathers have to do with anything?"

"Chickens have feathers," I said.

Cat giggled. "I know that," she said. "But so what? Is there a feather smuggler on the loose?"

"Kind of," said Sam. "There's a Gutman in the building, and the Gutmans now own a pillow company."

"Oh," said Egg and Cat together.

"So it looks like we have two suspects," I said. "Chuck the chicken fryer next door, and Anton Gutman for the feathers."

"I think we should add one more," Cat said. She nodded at a student leaning against the wall way in the back: Harriet.

"Harriet?" I asked. "Why would she be a suspect?"

"You heard all that stuff she said about the animals being unhappy," Cat said.

Sam nodded and pulled out her notebook to add Harriet's name to the list.

The central room had a huge glass and steel dome set into its ceiling. Sunlight streamed in through the dome, filling the giant room.

We stood just inside the doorway with the rest of the class. Dr. Flickenflak and Mr. Spade stood at the front of the group and waited for all of us to settle down.

When we were all quiet, Dr. Flickenflak said, "Here we have model skeletons of three of the largest dinosaurs we know of."

Her voice echoed through the room as she gestured toward the huge models behind her.

We'd seen them before, obviously. I bet any of the kids in Mr. Spade's class could recite the speech the doctor was giving — except Harriet and Jace. These three dinosaurs were the argentinosaurus, the spinosaurus, and the quetzalcoatlus.

The argentinosaurus is a huge thing on four legs, with a giant neck and tail. It's big and everything, but it's not very cool. The spinosaurus looks a little like a T. rex, except it's got a sail on its back and a long face. It's much cooler than the plant-eating argentinosaurus.

But my favorite is the quetzalcoatlus. It looks like a mix between a bat, a lizard, and a dragon.

The model is way high up, so it looks like the skeleton is soaring over the other two dinosaurs. When I was little, I was so scared of the quetzalcoatlus model that I ran out of the room and hid in the bathroom.

"Wow," said Jace. "This place is amazing!" He hurried to a bench near the wall and sat down. He pulled out his sketchbook while Dr. Flickenflak gave her dinosaur talk.

My friends and I had heard all about these dinosaurs before, so we found Anton in the crowd. He was snickering with his friends, looking at a display of fossilized dinosaur poop. I guess it *was* pretty funny.

Sam strode right up to Anton and his friends. She's not intimidated by anyone.

"Hello, dorks," Anton said as we stood around him and his friends.

"Anton," Sam replied with a nod.

"Don't tell me," he snarled. "Someone stole the chickens, and you're going to accuse me."

Sam crossed her arms. "You know an awful lot, don't you?" she said.

"What can I say?" Anton said. "I'm naturally gifted with beauty and brains."

"Ha!" I said. I couldn't help it. No one would use either of those words to describe Anton.

"If you know so much," Egg said, "maybe you know where your mom gets the feathers for her pillows." Egg used to be afraid of Anton. But lately, he's really learned to stand up to him — especially when he's with the three of us.

"Her pillows?" Anton stammered. He straightened up and forced a smile.

He turned to his goons. "Why don't you two take a walk?" he said. The boys grunted and snarled. They headed off to lean on a wall someplace.

"Listen," Anton said quietly. "It's none of your business where we get the feathers."

"You better talk, Gutman," Sam said. "There are some chickens missing, and chickens have feathers."

"Well, it wasn't my mom!" Anton said. "And it wasn't me! Mom gets her, um, feathers someplace . . . um . . ."

Just then, someone came up behind us. "Why are you four threatening my son?" came a shrill voice. We spun around, and there she was. A tall, skinny woman in a long, black coat with gold buttons, and with a bright, green scarf around her neck.

"Ms. Gutman?" Cat said.

"That's right," said Anton's mom. "Now please step away from my son."

The four of us backed up, and Anton hurried to his mom's side.

Sam wasn't bothered, though. She stepped right up to Ms. Gutman and said, "So, where do you get your feathers?"

"My feathers?" Anton's mom said. "What feathers?"

"The feathers for your pillows," Sam said.

"Oh," said Ms. Gutman, smiling. Her face went red. "Well . . . we have to keep some things secret. Otherwise every pillow maker in town will copy my recipe for success."

"So you don't deny that you use chicken feathers?" Sam said.

Ms. Gutman laughed. "Chicken feathers?" she said. "What are you talking about?"

"Why don't you catch your mom up on the morning's events," I said to Anton. "I am curious, though," I added, looking back at Anton's mom. "What are you doing here?"

"Why, I'm the parent chaperone on this trip," she said.

"Why weren't you on the bus?" Egg said. "Chaperones always ride the bus."

"Not that it's your business," she said, "but I was running late. I had an important business meeting this morning. After the meeting, I hopped into the company truck and got here as quickly as I could."

With that, the two Gutmans walked off.

"That didn't solve anything," I said.

"No," Sam said, scribbling in her notepad, "but she sure is acting suspiciously."

"Now what?" Egg said. He snapped a few photos of the giant dinosaur models and the rest of the class strolling around and looking at the bones.

Sam pointed at Harriet, who stood alone at the feet of the spinosaurus.

"Interrogation time?" Cat said with a sigh. "I hate interrogation time."

Sam put an arm around her shoulders. "Sorry, Cat," she said. "I think this one has to be all yours."

"Me?" Cat said. "Why me?"

"Because she's your friend," I put in. "You two already have so much in common."

"Gum has a point," said Sam. "You both love animals, right?"

"But you're on the right side of the law," Egg added.

"Hey," said Cat. "Harriet is innocent until proven guilty."

"True," Sam said. "So? You'll go talk to her?"

Cat took a deep breath. "Okay," she said. "But you three have to come with me and stay nearby. She . . . she kinda scares me a little."

"She *is* pretty tough," I agreed.

The four of us strolled toward Harriet. Egg, Sam, and I moved a little way off, where we could still hear everything, and Cat went right up to Harriet.

Cat smiled and put a brave face on. "Hi, Harriet," she said. "Pretty amazing, huh?"

"What?" said Harriet.

"The spinosaurus," Cat said. "It's so big."

"Oh, right," said Harriet. She shuffled her feet and picked at something on her coat.

Cat went right on smiling. "So," she said, "pretty cool about those chickens, huh?"

"What chickens?" asked Harriet.

"The ones that went missing from the aviary," Cat said. "I mean, they're free now, right? They're probably way happier."

Harriet shrugged. "Maybe," she said.

Cat leaned a little closer. "Did you free them?" she asked.

"If I freed the captive chickens," Harriet said, "do you think I'd tell you about it?"

"What?" asked Cat.

"You think I don't know what you're doing?" Harriet said. "With your crime-solving friends snooping nearby?"

Cat's smile drooped into a frown and she stared at her feet.

Harriet shook her head. "Honestly, Cat," she said. "I thought you were on our side. On the animals' side."

Then she stomped off.

"I am!" Cat said. "I am on your side!"

But Harriet was gone.

I hurried over to Cat and patted her shoulder. "It's okay," I said. "You did really well."

Sam nodded. "You sure did," she said. "Harriet was acting super guilty."

She pulled out her notebook as a shout rang out from the other end of the gallery.

"Bones are missing!" a voice called out.

A young woman came running through the gallery, dressed in the same white jumpsuit as the worker at the aviary. She ran right up to Dr. Flickenflak and shouted, "A dinosaur has been stolen!"

CHAPTER FIVE

LITTLE DINOSAUR

Anton started laughing. "The dinosaurs are right here," he said with glee. He pointed at the three giants under the dome ceiling.

"My son is right," said Ms. Gutman. "Why, it's laughable to even imagine someone trying to steal a dinosaur. One leg bone is bigger than I am!"

The woman in the white jumpsuit looked up at the giant models. "Not one of those," she said. "Not all dinosaurs were that big."

"Which model is missing?" asked Dr. Flickenflak.

"The mononykus, doctor," said the woman.

"Thank you, Andrea," said the doctor. "Please notify security right away." The woman in white hurried off.

Dr. Flickenflak strode across the gallery floor. The class and Mr. Spade followed. In front of a big window was a short, brown column. Only Jace stayed behind. He was still busy sketching the big dinos.

The glass case on top of the column was empty. A small placard read, "Mononykus." There was also a little drawing of what the dinosaur would have looked like. To me, it looked kind of like an emu.

"What's a mononykus?" Egg asked. "I've never heard of it."

MONONYKUS

"It's one of our newest models here at the museum," said the doctor. "It was much smaller than most of our models, as you can see. Still, it was very important to our exhibit." She was tapping her toes anxiously and wringing her hands. "Oh my, oh my."

"Was it worth a lot?" Egg asked.

"Dinosaur bones must be worth a fortune," Cat said.

The doctor smiled at her. "Most of our models aren't real dinosaur fossils or bones," she said. "They are plaster casts based on the bones scientists have found. Some of the casts are simply our best guess what a bone or a dinosaur looked like." She shook her head. "But the model was brand-new," she added. "It was purchased to go with the new aviary."

The doctor's phone rang, and she stepped away to answer it. My friends and I gathered to discuss the case.

"Well, that sure throws a monkey wrench in the works, doesn't it?" Sam said. She pulled out her notebook and started crossing everything out.

"What do you mean?" I asked.

"Two thefts in one day," she said. "One is of several live chickens. The other, a model of a dinosaur skeleton."

"So?" Cat asked.

"So," said Egg, "it's probably not a coincidence. And that rules out someone just trying to steal feathers, like Ms. Gutman."

"Or just trying to rescue chickens," Sam said, "like Harriet."

"Or get some free meat to cook," I added.

"So our suspect list," Cat concluded, "is now at zero again."

LUNCH

Lunchtime came too quickly for once. I love lunch, but when my friends and I are on a case, it can sometimes get in the way.

The class gathered in the museum cafeteria with our lunches. Harriet sat alone by the window and chomped on a celery stick. I could tell Cat was thinking about going over. But with the glares that Harriet was shooting at everyone, Cat just sat down with the three of us instead. I sure didn't blame her for that.

When we were all seated, Sam asked, "What's he up to?" She nodded over my shoulder, and I turned to see. It was Jace, the new artist, hunched over something at his table. He sure wasn't eating lunch.

"Let's find out," I said. I called over to him. "How's it going, Jace?"

He looked up, startled, and then saw me smiling at him. "Oh, hi," he said. "I'm just trying to finish this sketch."

I leaned across the aisle and looked over his shoulder. "Hey, that looks a little like the mononykus," I said. It was a long, lean, small skeleton. It kind of looked like a bird running — a bird without skin or feathers.

"The what?" Jace asked. He scraped his pencil across the paper, adding shading to a bone.

"The missing model," Egg said. "Were you sketching it in the main gallery?"

"I don't know what it was called," he said. "Why?"

"Well, if you were sketching it," Sam said as she stood up and leaned across our table, "maybe you saw something."

"Something?" Jace asked. He still didn't even look up from his drawing.

"Maybe you saw who grabbed it," Cat explained.

"Someone grabbed it?" Jace asked. "I don't know anything about that. I'm just annoyed that I didn't have time to finish my sketch."

Sam smiled. "I bet you wish you could take the models home with you, huh?" she said. "Then you'd have all the time you need."

Jace laughed and finally looked up. "Yeah, that would be great," he said. Then suddenly his face dropped. "Wait a minute," he said. "Hey, what are you saying?"

Sam threw up her hands. "Nothing at all," she said. "Enjoy your lunch." She sat down, opened her lunch bag, and pulled out a container of pasta salad.

I leaned over and whispered to her. "You don't think Jace stole the model, do you?" I asked.

"It makes sense," Egg said. "Look how big his bag is. Who else could fit a small dinosaur in their bag?"

Most of the other kids didn't even have a bag with them. Those that did just had little pocketbooks or book bags, nowhere near as big as Jace's artist's bag.

"There's one problem, though," Cat said. "Why would Jace steal a bunch of chickens?"

"And where would he put them?" I said.

"Exactly," Sam said. "Which means maybe we were wrong to think we were wrong."

"Huh?" said Egg, Cat, and I at the same time.

"The crimes," Sam said, poking at her pasta salad. "They're not related after all." She popped a noodle into her mouth and smiled as she chewed it.

"So there's no connection between the dinosaur and the chickens," Egg said.

"No connection at all," said Sam.

Then seemingly out of nowhere, a strange man leapt up to our table and cackled. We all turned toward him, alarmed.

"That's right!" he yelled. "There is no connection between dinosaurs and chickens. Tell your friends!"

He stood there a moment, his fists on his hips, and grinned at us. He was around Mr. Spade's age, with wild, orange hair under a hairnet. His clothes were stained and the same color as his hair.

"Um, hi," Cat said.

Just as quickly and oddly as he had appeared, he darted off, laughing and whooping and calling out, "There's no connection between dinosaurs and chickens!"

Egg snapped a bunch of photos before the man disappeared from the cafeteria.

"That was weird," I said as I pulled out my sandwich. "Ugh. Chicken salad."

SNOOPS

"Soon, we make our move," said Sam. The class headed down the west hallway toward the last stop of our visit: the planetarium.

"Under the cover of darkness, we can snoop around," she went on. We got in line at the theater doors with the rest of the class.

"Today's planetarium presentation is very special," Dr. Flickenflak said. "It is all about the asteroid that struck the earth sixty-five million years ago, all but wiping out the dinosaurs."

"Snoop around how?" Cat whispered as the doctor talked.

Sam whispered back to Cat, "You and Egg, check Jace's bag for plaster bones. Gum, you and I will sneak outside and look for Ms. Gutman's truck. We might find the chickens."

"And we might not," I said.

"It's our duty to look," Sam insisted. "While we're out there, we can check the chicken place next door."

"If it's not too late," Cat said. "If that Chuck guy took the chickens, he's probably already turned them into a ten-piece bucket!"

I laughed. I couldn't help it.

The line of students started to move inside the theater. As we entered, I spotted that weird guy from the cafeteria again.

"Dinosaurs and chickens?" the man said. "That's nuts!"

He said it over and over as the sixth graders moved past him. "Nuts, huh?" Anton said out of the side of his mouth to his goons. "He'd know!" He laughed like crazy. His goons sounded like chuckling hippos.

The four of us found seats near the exit. Luckily, Jace sat near the exit too. He had his sketchbook out for a moment, but then the lights went down. He leaned over and slipped it into his bag.

"We'll head out now," Sam whispered close to my ear. "Before the show starts." She turned to Cat on her other side. "You and Egg try to grab Jace's bag after the show starts, so he's distracted."

Cat nodded. Sam and I sneaked toward the door, staying as low as possible. I noticed Dr. Flickenflak was at the microphone, ready to start.

Mr. Spade stared at the curved screen on the ceiling, excited for the presentation. Ms. Gutman was already snoring.

Sam and I had no trouble sneaking out. We didn't get far after that, though. Instead we walked right into a burly security guard.

"Hey, where are you two kids going on your own?" he said. His voice was deep and rough.

Sam grabbed my arm. "When I count to three," she whispered out of the side of her mouth, "we make a run for the exit."

But I didn't think an escape was necessary. "Sorry, sir," I said before Sam could begin counting. "We're with Franklin Middle School."

"And?" the security guard asked.

"And," I replied, "our chaperone sent us out to her truck. She wants a pillow."

The guard's face lit up with a smile. "You mean Ms. Gutman?" he said. "*The* Ms. Gutman?"

Sam and I nodded.

"She makes the finest pillows ever!" he said. "Why, I don't think I could sleep at all if not for her wonderful pillows. I saw her truck right outside just a minute ago."

"Right out there?" I asked, pointing toward the side exit behind him.

"That's right," he said. "But I don't like the idea of you two going out of the building on your own. I'll escort you."

"Oh, that's not necessary," I said.

"I insist," said the guard, and he motioned us to start walking. "Besides," he added with a grin, "I'd love to get a look inside the back of Ms. Gutman's truck."

He marched us along the corridor toward the service exit. Sam leaned in and quietly said, "This could work out great."

"How so?" I asked.

"If the chickens are in there," she said, "the guard will think he solved the crime. He'll take her into custody."

"And if they're not?" I said.

She shrugged. "Then we grab a pillow for Ms. Gutman," she said, "and we hurry back to the planetarium."

"What about investigating Chuck's Cluck Cluck?" I said.

She chewed her bottom lip for a moment. When we reached the exit and the guard swung the door open for us, she said. "I'll think of something."

There was the truck. It had the same photo of a sleeping face, the same slogan, and the same big lettering that read "Gutman Pillows." It also had a big photo of Ms. Gutman herself, smiling and proud, in a fancy blue dress and pearl necklace. Along the bottom, it said "Stuffed with the finest materials!"

The guard walked with us right to the back door of the truck. Sam and I looked at the latch. Then we looked at each other and shrugged. Neither of us had any idea how to open it.

"Here, let me help you," the guard said. He leaned between us, grabbed the lever, and gave it a strong jerk. The truck's door flew up so fast that Sam and I jumped back. I even covered my eyes.

"I can't believe it," the guard said.

The chickens! I thought.

But when I opened my eyes, the back of the truck was full of nothing but pillows, as far as the eye could see.

"So many wonderful pillows," the guard said, sniffling. "It brings tears to my eyes."

"I was so sure they'd be here!" Sam said. She jumped up into the back of the truck and started digging among the pillows. I guess she was still hoping to find a cage of chickens.

"What are you talking about?" the guard said. "They are here! It's nothing but pillows."

"Huh?" Sam said, half buried in the pillows. "Oh, right. Pillows. Ha, it sure is! I'll just grab one." So she did, and then she hopped down.

"I'll get you two kids back inside," the guard said, still eyeing the pillows, probably wishing he could dive in and fall asleep right then and there.

"Thanks, sir," I said.

He closed the back of the truck and led the way across the sidewalk to the building's main entrance.

"Sorry, the side door locks on its own," he said as we walked.

As we got closer to the door, I spotted an orange blur bouncing around nearby. It was the wacky guy from the museum cafeteria.

I was about to nudge Sam to point him out when, to my surprise, the guard waved and called out to him, "Hi there, Chuck! How's the chicken business?"

Sam and I exchanged a wide-eyed glance. "There really is a Chuck at Chuck's Cluck Cluck?" I whispered.

Sam squinted at me. "I guess so," she said. "And that's him."

"It's been bad, Dave," Chuck replied, "ever since the new exhibit opened."

"Sorry to hear it," Dave said. He opened the big front doors for us and we hurried in, headed back to the planetarium theater.

"What does that mean?" I asked as we jogged down the hall.

"I'm not completely sure," Sam said, "but I think this case is coming to a close."

We slipped back into the theater as quietly as we could. As we passed Ms. Gutman's seat, we dropped the pillow in her lap.

"Where'd you get that?" Anton hissed at us. His mom didn't wake up, so we didn't bother answering him.

The presentation was nearly over. Sam and I sat in our seats next to Egg and Cat, who both shook their heads. They hadn't found anything in Jace's bag.

Sam and I weren't surprised. We had a new suspect. There was just one piece of information missing.

"After the asteroid hit," Dr. Flickenflak announced over the PA system, "dinosaurs were nearly extinct within just a few days. But they weren't all gone, were they?"

Some people mumbled in the audience. Did she mean there were still dinosaurs around today?

"No, they weren't all gone," the doctor went on. I could hear the smile in her voice. "Because dinosaurs live on today — as birds!"

As she said the word "birds," the theater doors flew open. The planetarium filled with light, and the class jumped up and shouted in confusion and surprise. Then came the orange blur again: Chuck the chicken man.

"Lies!" he shouted as he ran down the center aisle. "It's all lies!"

Chuck ran right to the middle and grabbed Dr. Flickenflak's microphone.

"Everything she told you is a lie," Chuck said. "Birds are birds! They're not dinosaurs!"

Dave the guard grabbed Chuck, Dr. Flickenflak took back the microphone, and Mr. Spade got the class quieted down.

"What exactly is going on here?" Dave asked.

Sam stood up. "I think we can explain," she said.

"We can?" asked Egg and Cat.

"That's Chuck," I whispered to them. "Chuck the chicken man."

I watched the gears turn in their heads. They'd figure it out in a minute. Meanwhile Sam would explain to everyone else.

"First," said Sam, "we thought the chickens had been taken for their meat."

"I would never!" Chuck interrupted. "My restaurant serves only the finest chickens, from the finest farms."

"She wasn't done," I said.

Sam cleared her throat and went on. "We also thought maybe someone wanted the chicken feathers," she said. She looked at Ms. Gutman, but she was still asleep.

"But both those theories went out the window," Sam said, "when the mononykus model was stolen."

Cat was getting it now. She stood up and picked up the explanation. "We figured the two thefts might not be connected," she said. "In fact, we knew one person would love to get his hands on a dinosaur skeleton model." She glanced at Jace.

"I didn't steal anything," said Jace, jumping out of his seat.

"We know," said Cat. "I checked your bag."

"You what?" Jace said.

"We're so sorry," Cat said. Then she smiled. "I really liked your drawings, though. You're a great artist."

"Oh," said Jace, and then his face went red. "Thanks."

"When Sam and I saw Chuck outside," I said, "and realized he was the same man who'd been shouting in the cafeteria about dinosaurs and chickens, the whole thing clicked into place."

"The dinosaur theft," Sam said, "and the missing chickens were related."

Dave looked at me and Sam, and then at Chuck. "I don't get it," the guard said.

"I don't either," Chuck said. "What could some missing chickens have to do with a dinosaur?"

"I can answer that," said Dr. Flickenflak. "All modern birds are actually descended from dinosaurs — even the chicken is really a dinosaur. The smaller dinosaurs were like modern birds in many ways. Several even had feathers."

"More lies!" Chuck said.

"Lies, huh?" Sam said. "Follow us." She headed up the main aisle, so Egg, Cat, and I followed. Soon the rest of the class, Dave the guard, Dr. Flickenflak, and Chuck the chicken man followed too.

"Where are we going?" Chuck called out from the back. He found out soon enough. Sam led us out the main doors and right into Chuck's Cluck Cluck chicken restaurant.

"What's the meaning of this?" Chuck protested, but Sam didn't stop. She went right into the back of the shop.

"Aha!" she called out, so of course the rest of us ran to the back too. There, among the fryers and prep tables full of vegetables and cheese, were a cage full of chickens and a perfect model of the skeleton of a mononykus.

"Where's Chuck?" asked Dave. The chicken man wasn't in the back room with us. A bell dinged. Someone was heading out the shop's front door.

Dave the guard took off like a shot. My friends and I followed. Chuck darted down the sidewalk — right into Ms. Gutman, still holding her super-fluffy pillow. Dave was able to grab Chuck's collar. The chicken man had nowhere to go now.

Dave took off his cap. "Thank you, Ms. Gutman," he said. He blushed and helped her to her feet. "I'm a big fan."

"Why thank you, officer," she said. "Please, accept this pillow."

I've never seen a happier security guard. "I'll cherish it," he said. Then he put handcuffs on Chuck.

"Chuck, I don't get it," the guard said. "I know business hasn't been good, but what did you hope to gain by stealing some chickens and dinosaur bones?"

"I won't talk without my lawyer here," Chuck said.

"It's simple," I said. "Chuck the chicken man thought that if people knew chickens were descended from dinosaurs, they wouldn't want to eat his food."

Cat nodded. "I think he's right," she said.

"See?" Chuck said. "I knew it. My business is ruined."

"It is not," I said. "Cat's already a vegetarian. She was never going to eat your chicken, whether it was made of dinosaurs or earthworms."

"Gross," said Cat.

"Now, if you ask me," I went on, "I'm even more excited about eating some chicken."

"Huh?" said Chuck.

"Me too," said Sam. "Who would've thought I'd be eating deep-fried dinosaur on a roll with cheese?"

Egg laughed. "Totally!" he said. "Serve me a bucket of T. rex!" Sam and I laughed at that. Cat wasn't amused.

"Wait a minute," Chuck said, calling out to the whole class. "Do you other kids feel the same way?"

Everyone cheered — everyone except Cat and Harriet, anyway.

"This is wonderful news!" said Chuck. "I'll make it the heart of my marketing. We'll serve Dino Nuggets, and Sandwichosaurs, and Pteranodon Buffalo Wings!"

He was really on a roll. "I'll even change the name from Chuck's Cluck Cluck to Chuck Dore's Cluck Cluck Roar!" he shouted.

He was so excited, his face was red and his smile was huge. He was so happy, even, that he forgot he was wearing handcuffs. Dave the guard reminded him.

"I'm sure it'll be a huge success," Dave said, pulling Chuck to the police car that had pulled up at the curb. "You can make all those changes once you get out of prison."

"Chuck was no sitting duck, but now he's out of luck," I joked as we headed back to the museum. "And all that prison food will make him say 'yuck!'"

Sam groaned. "That's enough, Gum."

"Sorry, Sam," I said with a grin. "You're stuck."

literary news

MYSTERIOUS WRITER REVEALED!

Steve Brezenoff lives in Minneapolis, Minnesota, with his wife, Beth and their son, Sam. Besides writing books, he enjoys playing video games, riding his bicycle, and helping middle-school students work on their writing skills. Steve's ideas almost always come to him in his dreams, so he does his best writing in his pajamas.

arts & entertainment

ARTIST IS KEY TO SOLVING MYSTERY, SAY POLICE

Marcos Calo lives happily in A Coruña, Spain, with his wife, Patricia (who is also an illustrator), and their daughter, Claudia. When Marcos and Patricia aren't drawing, they like to go on long walks by the sea. They also watch a lot of films and eat Nutella sandwiches. Yum!

A Detective's Dictionary

asteroid (ASS-tuh-roid)—a very small planet that travels around the sun

chaperone (SHAP-uh-rohn)—an adult who protects the safety of young people at an event such as a class trip

coincidence (koh-IN-si-duhnss)—a chance happening

exhibit (eg-ZIB-it)—a public show or display

innocent (IN-uh-suhnt)—not guilty

interrogation (in-ter-uh-GAY-shun)—detailed questioning

intimidated (in-TIM-uh-date-id)—frightened

obvious (OB-vee-uhss)—easy to see or understand

paleontologist (pale-ee-uhn-TOL-uh-jist)—a scientist of fossils and other ancient life

planetarium (plan-uh-TAIR-ee-uhm)—a building with equipment for reproducing the position and movement of the sun, moon, planets, and stars by projecting their images onto a curved ceiling

protests (PROH-tests)—demonstrations against something

suspects (SUH-spekts)—people thought to have done a crime

suspiciously (suh-SPISH-uhss-lee)—in a distrustful way

James Shoo
6th Grade

Dinosaurs and Birds

When I heard Dr. Flickenflak say that birds were actually related to dinosaurs, I didn't know if I believed her.

It turns out I am not the only person to have doubts. Many scientists are not sure if there is a connection. However, recent discoveries make it seem more likely than ever.

There are many features that connect birds and a type of dinosaur called theropods. Theropods had similar leg and foot structures to birds, and they walked upright on two legs.

They also laid eggs, and their bones were interlaced with vessels. In some cases, the dinos even had feathers.

The mononykus, the dinosaur that disappeared on our field trip, was just one of more than a dozen birdlike dinos. It roamed the Earth about 72 million years ago and ate insects as its main food. Some scientists actually argue that it wasn't a dinosaur, though. They say it was a bird!

Well done, James. What do you think? Are birds and dinos connected? Mr. S.

FURTHER INVESTIGATIONS

CASE #FTM19JSNHM

1. Why do you think schools often take kids to natural history museums for their field trips?

2. List all the suspects in this case. Did any of the suspects seem more guilty than others? Talk about your reasoning.

3. Have you ever been to a natural history museum? What is your favorite section? Talk about it.

IN YOUR OWN DETECTIVE'S NOTEBOOK . . .

1. Gum wasn't too excited about this field trip. Have you ever had to go on a field trip that you didn't look forward to? How did it turn out?

2. In this book, Anton's mom was a chaperone. Has your parent ever chaperoned one of your field trips? Did you like having him or her chaperone?

3. This book is a mystery. Write your own mystery story.